I SEE GOD IN HIM

LIVIA XIA WANG

Made with ♥ on the Notion Press Platform
www.notionpress.com

To my beloved family, whose unwavering support and
boundless love have been my guiding light.

To my friends, who inspire me with their wisdom,
kindness, and encouragement.

To the readers, whose passion for stories breathes life into
my words.

And to those who have experienced the transformative
power of love and devotion, may you find strength and
solace in these pages.

This book is for you.

Contents

Preface

Dear Reader,

Welcome to a journey that delves into the intricate tapestry of human emotions, relationships, and the shadows that lurk within society. "I Saw God in You" is a story born from my deep-seated desire to explore the complexities of love, trust, and the fight for justice against insidious forces.

As an author, my goal is to create narratives that resonate with the heartstrings, stories that stay with you long after the final page is turned. This book, in particular, weaves together elements of crime investigation, the stark reality of human trafficking, and the profound love that can emerge even in the darkest of times.

Through the pages of this book, you will follow the protagonist's harrowing journey, filled with suspense, emotional upheaval, and an unwavering quest for truth and justice. It is my hope that this story will not only entertain but also provoke thought and empathy, shedding light on issues that often remain hidden in the shadows.

Thank you for choosing to embark on this journey with me. Your presence as a reader means the world, and I am deeply grateful for your time and attention.

With heartfelt gratitude,

Livia Xia Wang

Acknowledgements

First and foremost, I would like to express my deepest gratitude to my family. Your unwavering support and encouragement have been the foundation of my journey as a writer. To my beloved husband, thank you for your endless patience and understanding during the countless hours I spent lost in my writing. Your love and support have been my anchor.

To my children, your boundless energy and enthusiasm remind me daily of the importance of perseverance and passion. You are my greatest inspiration.

A heartfelt thank you to my friends, both old and new, who have stood by me through this creative journey. Your feedback, encouragement, and belief in my stories have been invaluable.

I would also like to extend my sincere appreciation to the incredible team at Notion Press. Your expertise and dedication have brought my vision to life in ways I could never have imagined. Thank you for guiding me through the publishing process and for believing in my work.

To my fellow writers and mentors, thank you for your wisdom, guidance, and camaraderie. The writing community has been a source of immense support and inspiration.

Lastly, to my readers, thank you for taking the time to read my stories. Your feedback and appreciation fuel my passion for writing. It is your connection to my characters and narratives that makes this journey worthwhile.

With heartfelt thanks,
Livia Xia Wang.

CHAPTER I

Introduction

Udham Sharma embodies a paradoxical existence: by day, a revered Senator known for his kindness and dedication to public service, and by night, a clandestine figure wielding influence in Mumbai's underworld. Raised in a family steeped in public service, Udham's ascent into politics was natural, driven by his intelligence and genuine empathy. His speeches resonate with eloquence and compassion, advocating tirelessly for social reforms in education and healthcare. Yet, behind this facade lies a carefully concealed reality—Udham's deep involvement in criminal circles .

In the criminal underworld, Udham manages his operations with careful accuracy and practical approaches.His dual life is a constant tightrope walk, balancing the demands of his legitimate political career with the necessity of preserving his underworld connections. Despite the moral complexities, Udham's commitment to his family remains unwavering. He shields them from the dangers of his hidden activities while grappling with the ethical dilemmas posed by his contrasting roles. His family remains unaware of his criminal background.

Aarav Sharma, the only son of Udham Sharma, was born into privilege but raised in profound loneliness. His mother's untimely death during childbirth left him emotionally adrift, lacking the nurturing care a child craves. Udham, consumed by his dual life as a Senator and underworld figure, provided Aarav with material comforts but was often absent emotionally, leaving him to navigate his formative years surrounded by superficial friendships that revolved around his wealth.

Despite his charming demeanor, Aarav struggled with a profound sense of emptiness. He yearned for genuine connection and love, seeking solace in relationships that often proved disappointing. His trust in Mitra, his ex-girlfriend, was shattered when she too betrayed him, deepening his emotional wounds. With each betrayal, Aarav withdrew further into himself, disillusioned and questioning the authenticity of human relationships.

In college, Aarav's outward charm masked his inner turmoil. His rebellious behavior and disregard for consequences earned him a reputation that belied his true desire for acceptance and understanding. Frustration and depression became constant companions as he grappled with the disparity between his outward appearance and inner turmoil. Despite his longing for happiness, Aarav found himself trapped in a cycle of disillusionment, unsure of how to break free and find genuine fulfillment in a world that seemed indifferent to his emotional needs.

Aditya Verma was renowned in police circles as an astute and dedicated investigator with an uncanny ability to uncover the intricate webs spun by criminals like Udham Sharma. As an undercover officer, Aditya immersed himself in the shadows of Mumbai's underworld, gathering intelligence and piecing together fragments of information that hinted at Udham's elusive activities. Despite his intuitive understanding of Udham's operations, concrete evidence remained elusive, frustrating his efforts to bring the Senator to justice.

Aditya's investigation was a covert mission, known to only a select few trusted colleagues who understood the risks involved. He navigated the dangerous terrain of organized crime with meticulous caution, aware that any misstep could jeopardize not only his career but also his life. His persistence and determination to uncover the truth drove him forward, even as the shadows grew darker and the risks escalated.

Tragically, Aditya's pursuit of justice came to an abrupt and unforeseen end. While following a crucial lead in Udham Sharma's case, Aditya met his demise in a mysterious accident that silenced his voice and left his investigation unfinished. The circumstances surrounding his death raised suspicions and fueled speculation, but the truth of his findings remained buried with him. Aditya's passing left a void in the law enforcement community, a poignant reminder of the perilous nature of the pursuit of justice in the face of formidable adversaries like Udham Sharma.

Ishan Verma grew up in the shadow of his father's legacy, Aditya Verma, a revered police investigating officer whose dedication to justice had left an indelible mark on him. Raised with a deep sense of integrity and responsibility, Ishan admired his father's unwavering commitment to truth and fairness. The loss of his father in the line of duty was a profound blow, but Ishan found solace in his mother's strength and perseverance, as she secured a government job following her husband's tragic death.

From a young age, Ishan was drawn to the world of law enforcement, inspired by his father's heroic tales and driven by a desire to follow in his footsteps. His upbringing instilled in him a strong moral compass and a deep empathy for those affected by crime and injustice. Despite the pain of his loss, Ishan channeled his grief into determination, dedicating himself to becoming a skilled and respected investigation officer like his father.

As Ishan entered the police force, his youthful energy and unwavering determination quickly earned him recognition among his peers. His sharp intellect and ability to connect with people made him a natural in investigative work, while his genuine empathy and compassion set him apart. Ishan's main focus became unraveling the mysteries surrounding his father's unfinished cases, driven by a personal quest to uncover the truth and bring closure to his family and his father's legacy.

While navigating the complexities of his chosen profession, Ishan never forgot the lessons imparted by his father—to uphold justice without compromise and to protect the innocent. His bond with his mother remained a pillar of strength, their mutual support and love serving as constants in a world often marked by uncertainty and danger. With each step forward in his career, Ishan honored his father's memory, determined to make a difference in the lives of those he served and to fulfill the unfinished mission that had defined Aditya Verma's life and legacy.

Ishan Verma, now operating under the alias Varun Kulkarni, is on a critical mission investigating the surge of missing girl cases in and around Mumbai. The police department, suspecting Udham Sharma's involvement, devised a strategic plan to infiltrate his inner circle through his son, Aarav. Disguised as a college student, Ishan's objective is to befriend Aarav and gather intelligence to expose Udham's underworld operations. Despite Aarav's ignorance of his father's illicit dealings, his innate sense that something is amiss provides Ishan with an opening. As Varun Kulkarni, Ishan must navigate the dangerous path of undercover work, balancing the genuine bond forming with Aarav against the relentless pursuit of justice, all while honoring his late father's legacy and determination to bring the truth to light.

The story is unfolding through the unforgettable experiences that have occurred in Aarav's life.

CHAPTER II

The Abyss of Uncertainty

In the quiet solitude of his dimly lit room, Aarav Sharma poured his heart onto the screen of his laptop, capturing fragments of his story that transcended mere words. Each keystroke echoed the depths of his soul, weaving a narrative that unfolded like a tapestry of memories and emotions.

"I saw God in him," Aarav began, his fingers dancing with a mix of nostalgia and reverence.

I woke abruptly to the jarring news that Mitra, my former girlfriend, was missing. The weight of disbelief and concern settled heavily upon me as I struggled to comprehend the gravity of the situation. Despite our romantic ties being severed, the bond we once shared lingered in the recesses of my heart, prompting a surge of anxious curiosity about her well-being.

At first, I hesitated to search for her. Mitra had deceived me in a way that left deep scars—she had manipulated me into giving her large sums of money under false pretenses, claiming it was for emergencies and important needs. In reality, she used the money to live a lavish lifestyle, all while pretending to love me. When I finally realized the extent of her deception, I cut ties with her, feeling betrayed and heartbroken.

However, a sense of humanitarian duty and a concern for appearances weighed on me. If I didn't look into her disappearance, people might suspect I had taken revenge. Reluctantly, I decided to search for her, driven by these concerns and the faint hope of uncovering the truth about her fate.

The previous night was a haze of blurred memories and disorientation. I had spent it in the company of friends at our favorite bar, seeking solace in harmony and the fleeting distraction of laughter. Yet, as details began to trickle in, I learned from my maid that an unfamiliar face had escorted me home in my intoxicated state—a night lost to the oblivion of intoxication.

With each passing moment, a whirlwind of questions and uncertainties swirled in my mind. Where was Mitra? What had happened during those foggy hours that now seemed so distant and elusive?

As I grappled with the unfolding mystery, a pang of regret pierced through my haze of confusion. Despite the complexities of our past, Mitra's absence cast a stark light on the unresolved emotions and unfinished conversations between us. In this unexpected moment of crisis, my longing to unravel the truth intertwined with a desperate hope for her safe return, overshadowing any traces of our fractured relationship.

It was already too late to make it to college on time. Hastily, I grabbed my bag and rushed out the door, skipping breakfast in my urgency to piece together the events of the previous night and uncover any clues about Mitra's disappearance. The streets were a blur as I navigated through the bustling city, my mind racing with a mix of apprehension and determination.

Arriving at college, I found myself distracted, unable to focus on lectures or assignments. Every passing minute felt like an eternity as I anxiously awaited any news or developments. My friends noticed my preoccupation, offering concerned glances and sympathetic gestures, but my thoughts remained consumed by the mystery surrounding Mitra.

Throughout the day, I oscillated between hope and fear, grappling with the uncertainty of her whereabouts and the weight of my own fragmented memories. Each unanswered question deepened my resolve to uncover the truth, pushing me to retrace my steps and seek out anyone who might shed light on the events leading up to Mitra's disappearance.

As evening descended, I found myself back at home, restless and haunted by the lingering echoes of that fateful night. With a sense of urgency gnawing at my conscience, I resolved to delve deeper into the enigma that now overshadowed my every thought, determined to unravel the mystery and find closure for both Mitra and myself.

CHAPTER III

A Glimmer of Trust

It was at that moment, my maid mentioned, the boy who had taken me home had come by in the morning to leave some hangover remedies.

"Why didn't you tell me earlier?" I inquired, a mix of curiosity and frustration in his voice.

"You were in such a rush this morning. I couldn't get a chance. I'm sorry," the maid replied, her tone apologetic.

"Did you get any details about him?" I asked, my curiosity piqued.

"Yes, he said he knows you. His name is Varun Kulkarni. He's a student in the communicative English course," she explained.

"Varun Kulkarni?" I repeated, trying to place the name.

"Yes, that's right," the maid assured me.

I took the drink and retreated to my room. As I examined the bottle, I noticed a note taped to it: "Drink this before you come to college."

I smiled, feeling a rare warmth. It had been a long time since anyone showed me genuine care. As I drank, I noticed a small sticker at the bottom with Varun's phone number and the message, "Call me if you need anything." My smile widened as I noted the number and dialed.

"It's me, Aarav. Thank you for yesterday and for the drink. I'm sorry for any trouble I caused," I said, my voice sincere.

"Oh, it's no big deal. I'm always ready to help," Varun replied with a warm smile, while silently thinking, "What I've been searching for all along has finally come to me."

"Why are you helping me? I don't know you. You're a stranger," I asked, suspicion lacing his words.

"Well then, let's change that. I'll meet you tomorrow on campus. Lunch is on me. I'll call you," Varun replied, a hint of a smile in his voice.

"See you, Varun," I said, about to disconnect.

"Wow, you know my name," Varun noted with a chuckle.

"Of course, the maid told me," I responded, smiling.

"Oh, cool. Well then, see you tomorrow," Varun said, disconnecting the call with a knowing smile.

I hung up, feeling a strange sense of anticipation. For the first time in a long while, someone had reached out with genuine kindness, and it stirred something hopeful within me.

The next day, I felt an unusual sense of anticipation as I got ready for college. Despite the lingering worries about Mitra's disappearance, the prospect of meeting

Varun brought a flicker of curiosity and hope. He made his way to campus, feeling slightly more optimistic than he had in a while.

As promised, Varun called around lunchtime. "Hey Aarav, ready for lunch?" Varun's voice was cheerful, a stark contrast to my usual interactions.

"Yeah, where should we meet?" I asked.

"Let's meet at the campus café. It's quiet and the food's pretty good," Varun suggested.

I agreed and headed to the café. I spotted Varun at a corner table, waving him over with a friendly smile. Varun was casually dressed, his demeanor easygoing and approachable.

"Hey, Aarav! Over here," Varun called out as I approached.

"Hey, thanks for the invite," I said, taking a seat opposite Varun.

"No problem at all. You seemed like you could use a friend," Varun replied, his eyes warm with sincerity. "What do you want to eat? My treat."

They ordered their meals, and as they waited, an easy conversation flowed. Varun had a knack for making me feel at ease, asking about his interests, classes, and sharing stories from his own life. I found myself laughing and opening up more than I had in a long time.

"So, tell me about yesterday," Varun prompted gently. "What happened after we left the bar?"

I hesitated for a moment, then decided to be honest. "Honestly, it's all a blur. I don't remember much after a certain point. But I woke up to find out that Mitra, my ex, is missing. It's been...a lot to process."

Varun listened intently, his expression thoughtful. "I'm really sorry to hear that, Aarav. That must be incredibly tough. If there's anything I can do to help, just let me know."

I nodded, appreciating the offer. "Thanks, Varun. It means a lot. Honestly, just having someone to talk to helps."

Their food arrived, and the conversation shifted to lighter topics. Varun's easygoing nature made it effortless for me to relax. Over the course of the meal, I felt a connection forming, a tentative bond that offered a glimmer of hope amidst his current turmoil.

As they finished lunch, Varun leaned back in his chair, his eyes thoughtful. "You know, sometimes it's easier to face tough situations with someone by your side. If you ever need anything, even just to talk, I'm here."

I looked at Varun, genuinely touched. "Thanks, Varun. I appreciate it. Really."

"Anytime," Varun replied with a smile. "Now, let's get through the rest of this day and take it one step at a time."

As we parted ways, I felt a weight lift slightly off my shoulders. For the first time in a long while, I felt less alone.

Unknown to me, Varun was just as committed to uncovering the truth, his dual mission intertwined with a blooming friendship that would soon be tested by the complexities of their hidden agendas.

CHAPTER IV

Undercover Machinations

The next day, Varun approached me with a determined look, holding a folder with some information he had managed to gather about Mitra. My heart raced with a mix of hope and dread as I saw Varun walking towards me.

"I found some leads about Mitra," Varun said, handing over the folder. I quickly opened it, eager to find any clue about her whereabouts.

"Mitra was last seen leaving a session at the beauty salon," Varun began. "The salon's CCTV footage shows her taking the keys to her car and heading towards the parking lot. Unfortunately, the area where she parked wasn't covered by any cameras."

My face fell slightly, but I listened intently as Varun continued.

"However, we did find some useful footage from other cameras in the area, including dash cams," Varun said, pointing to some still images in the folder. "A lot of cars were seen leaving the parking lot around the time Mitra disappeared, but her car was not among them. It just vanished, along with her."

My mind raced with questions. "What does this mean? How could her car just disappear like that?"

"It's possible someone took her car and drove it to another location, or maybe she was forced into another vehicle," Varun suggested. "The fact that her car wasn't seen leaving the lot is concerning, but it gives us a timeframe to work with."

I nodded, feeling a mixture of frustration and determination. "So, what's the next step?"

"We need to check if any other cameras in the vicinity caught something we missed," Varun replied. "There might be gaps in the footage we haven't looked at yet. Also, we can start questioning people who were around the parking lot at that time. Someone might have seen something."

I felt a surge of gratitude towards Varun. Despite barely knowing him, he was going out of his way to help. "Thank you, Varun. I don't know what I would do without your help."

Varun smiled reassuringly. "We're in this together, Aarav. We'll find her."

As we continued to discuss our plan, I felt a sense of purpose I hadn't felt in a long time. With Varun's support, I was ready to do whatever it took to uncover the truth and bring Mitra back.

Later that evening, I sat in my dimly lit room, unable to shake the thoughts racing through my mind. I picked up my phone and sent Varun a message, curiosity and suspicion gnawing at me.

"I'm curious about why you're helping me this much?" I typed and hit send.

A few moments later, Varun's reply came in. "While we were talking yesterday, I felt like I should help you. Yes, I know from fellow students that your dad has a very strong influence, but you're not on good terms with him. Because of your previous misbehaviors, nobody dares to befriend you except for some who exploit you. You know that as well. But you need someone or something to hang on to, so you keep them around. Should I tell you more?"

My heart pounded as I read the message. How did Varun know so much about me? I quickly typed back, "How do you know me this well? Who are you actually?"

Varun's response was swift and reassuring. "I am one of your admirers. Just keep in mind that I'm not your enemy. You can trust me, and I will help you. Like you, I also want to know what happened to Mitra. Let's move together and make this a secret operation. You know that the police are also investigating the case."

I read Varun's message carefully, my mind a swirl of thoughts. His words carried a certain weight, a mix of understanding and sincerity. I realized that if I wanted to get to the bottom of Mitra's disappearance, I would need allies I could trust, even if I didn't fully understand their motives just yet.

"Alright, Varun. Let's do this together. I trust you," I typed back, hoping I was making the right decision.

Varun's response came swiftly, his tone filled with assurance. "Absolutely. Let's work this out. How about I swing by your place tomorrow? We can strategize our next moves face-to-face."

I considered for a moment, then replied, "Hmm... Sure."

"Perfect. Looking forward to it," Varun said warmly.

I sent him a thumbs up emoji, expressing my agreement and anticipation for our meeting.

As I put down my phone, I felt a mixture of apprehension and hope. For the first time in a long while, I wasn't facing my troubles alone. With Varun's help, I felt a renewed sense of purpose and determination to uncover the truth about Mitra's disappearance and confront the shadowy secrets that surrounded me.

The next day, Varun arrived at my house as planned. His car rolled to a stop outside, and I felt a surge of determination mixed with caution.

I welcomed him in, grateful for the support and eager to discuss our strategy for finding Mitra. Varun maintained a calm demeanor, hiding his true intentions behind a façade of friendship and concern.

As we settled in the living room, I retrieved some refreshments while Varun subtly observed his surroundings. He noted the layout of the house, the security measures in place, and my unsuspecting demeanor.

"I've been thinking," Varun began casually, "we should consider all angles in our search for Mitra. Sometimes, the answers might be closer than we think."

I nodded in agreement, eager for any leads. "Yeah, I've been wracking my brain trying to figure out where she could have gone."

Varun maintained his cool exterior, masking his inner resolve to uncover the truth about my father. "What if we start by understanding more about your dad's influence? Maybe he knows something that could help."

I hesitated, my expression clouding slightly. "I'm not sure how much he'd be willing to share. We haven't exactly been close. You know that."

Varun nodded sympathetically, concealing his true motives. "It's worth a shot. Trust me, sometimes parents surprise us."

As we continued our conversation, Varun subtly excused himself to use the restroom, taking the opportunity to discreetly explore the house. He kept a keen eye out for my father's office, knowing that accessing it without my knowledge was crucial.

After a brief search, Varun located the office nestled on the second floor, its door securely locked. With deft precision, he employed a sophisticated code reader to bypass the lock, the mechanism yielding smoothly to his touch. Swift and silent, he navigated the space, strategically placing hidden cameras and discreet recording devices in carefully chosen positions. Each movement was executed with a blend of practiced skill and focused determination, his heart pulsing with a rush of adrenaline as he meticulously ensured that every piece of equipment was concealed with expert finesse.

Once he completed his task, Varun rejoined me, his amiable facade masking the weight of his covert endeavor. As we stood together, I couldn't help but inquire about the delay, explaining that I had been engrossed in scouring the internet for updates on Mitra. Varun's response was delivered with a casual ease, yet I sensed an undercurrent of significance in his words—he had received a call from his mother, a simple explanation that seemed to carry deeper implications.

As we wrapped up our meeting, Varun suggested we reconvene soon to discuss any new leads. I agreed, thanking Varun for his dedication and support. Little did I know, Varun's true mission was set in motion, with secrets and revelations waiting to unfold in the shadows of my own home.

As my father arrived home unexpectedly, Varun subtly steered the conversation towards Mitra, observing his reactions with keen interest. He noted the slight flicker in Mr. Sharma's eyes, a brief moment of hesitation that didn't escape Varun's scrutiny. My father composed himself quickly, asserting confidently that the authorities were diligently working on finding Mitra.

"I've been pressuring them as well to do everything necessary," my father added, his voice carrying a hint of authority.

Varun nodded sympathetically, masking his suspicion with a deliberate compliment. "It's so admirable how involved you are, Mr. Sharma. I've heard that you're not just a successful businessman but also a kind-hearted person who helps those in need."

My father smiled warmly at the praise, his demeanor briefly softened. He placed a reassuring hand on Varun's shoulder before excusing himself to his office, leaving Varun to ponder the hidden depths behind his facade.

As Varun prepared to leave, he seized the opportunity to discreetly plant a GPS locator under my father's car. With practiced precision, he ensured the device was well-hidden, knowing that it could provide crucial insights into my father's movements and activities.

With the covert mission accomplished, Varun bid farewell to me, maintaining his friendly demeanor while internally processing the revelations of the day. His interactions with my father had only deepened his resolve to uncover the truth about Mitra's disappearance and to understand the extent of my father's involvement, both as a concerned father and potentially as a figure with hidden agendas in the underworld.

As Varun walked away from my house, the weight of secrecy and intrigue hung heavy on his mind. He knew that navigating the complexities of my family dynamics and my father's secretive world would require careful strategy and unwavering determination. Each step forward brought him closer to unraveling the tangled web of mysteries that threatened the safety of those entangled in my father's shadowy dealings.

Varun realizes that the GPS locator on Mr. Sharma's car is not yielding any significant leads. It becomes clear that Mr. Sharma is not directly involved in Mitra's disappearance, as he would not have used his own car for such a nefarious act. Varun understands that he needs to explore other avenues to solve this mystery.

Varun's investigation takes a new turn as he delves deeper into the world of human trafficking. He learns that human traffickers often operate without leaving a trace, using sophisticated methods to avoid detection. Unlike traditional kidnappings, human trafficking does not rely on direct contact with victims through messages or phone calls. Instead, traffickers often target young individuals indiscriminately, snatching them away from their lives without warning.

As Varun unravels the complexities of human trafficking, he realizes that Mitra's disappearance may be linked to a larger network of criminals. Determined to find her, Varun dives deeper into the underworld, leveraging his contacts and resources to uncover the truth.

Through his investigation, Varun encounters various challenges and dangers. He must navigate through a web of deceit and danger, where one wrong move could cost him everything. But fueled by his determination to bring Mitra home safely, Varun presses on, determined to unravel the mystery and bring those responsible to justice.

CHAPTER V

Revelations and Resolutions

As Udham Sharma , my dad, urgently conversed with his assistant, his anxiety caused him to neglect locking his office door. Passing by, I inadvertently caught snippets of their discussion. My father's tense tone and the troubling words I managed to overhear sent a chill down my spine. He seemed suspicious of Ishan and me searching for Mitra, issuing numerous instructions to his men. In that moment, I glimpsed another, more ominous side of my father. Overwhelmed with fear and disbelief, I quietly retreated to my room, my heart pounding with apprehension.

Inside the confines of my father's once-familiar office, fear gripped me like a vice as I dialed Varun's number in haste, my voice trembling with urgency. "Varun," I managed to choke out amidst tears, "I overheard my dad. He's tangled up in something horrifying. I never thought he could be capable of this. I'm terrified to stay here. Can I come to your place? Please, I need your help." Each word quivered with the weight of my distress, my entire being shaken to the core by the stark reality of my father's dark secrets.

Varun's heart sank. He knew the time had come for action. "Of course, I'll come and pick you up right away. Pack your things and get out before your dad notices," he replied urgently.

I hurriedly packed a bag, my hands shaking. Every sound in the house seemed amplified, my fear intensifying with each passing second. I managed to slip out undetected, my heart racing. Varun was waiting outside, his car engine running.

"You came so quick," I said, my voice still trembling.

"I was nearby," Varun replied, trying to sound casual. But I noticed something in Varun's eyes—an unease that I couldn't quite place.

"Is everything alright?" I asked, a note of suspicion creeping into my voice.

Varun hesitated, knowing that he couldn't hide the truth much longer. Taking me to his place would inevitably expose his true identity—his uniforms, his equipment, everything. Yet, leaving me at his and my house were equally dangerous. Udham Sharma's connections with a dangerous mafia, operating internationally, made any delay perilous.

Varun made a quick decision. "It's safer if we go to a hotel for now," he said, starting the car.

"Why are we going to a hotel? What's going on?" I inquired, my anxiety growing.

"I need to tell you something, but not here. It's not safe. Let's talk inside the hotel room," Varun said, his tone serious.

I nodded, though my mind was swirling with questions and fears. As we drove, I tried to process the rapid series of events, my hands clenched tightly in my lap. "When I thought I should do something for Mitra and you were helping me, I never knew we were in this much trouble. Now I feel completely lost," I said, my voice breaking as tears welled up in my eyes.

Varun reached over and held my hand briefly, his grip firm and reassuring. "Relax. Whatever it is, we'll face it together. Okay?" he said, his voice steady and calming.

Soon we reached the hotel, a nondescript building on the edge of town. Varun booked a room and we checked in, moving quickly to avoid any unwanted attention. Once inside the room, Varun locked the door and turned to me.

"Give me your phone," Varun said. I handed it over without question. Varun quickly installed a GPS tracker on the device.

"Please, tell me what's going on," I pleaded, my voice cracking.

Varun took a deep breath, steeling himself for the conversation ahead. "I need to be honest with you, even if it's difficult. My real name is Ishan Verma, and I'm an undercover detective from the CID. I'm sorry I couldn't reveal this to you earlier, but now it's crucial for you to know the truth."

My eyes widened in shock, but I stayed silent, listening intently.

"I've been investigating a case involving missing girls in and around Mumbai," Ishan began earnestly, his voice carrying a weight of honesty and regret. "I needed to get close to you to gather information about your father. Unfortunately, it turns out he's involved in this case. I knew about it before you did. But because it's a covert operation, I couldn't disclose anything to you. I'm truly sorry, Aarav. I never intended to deceive you, but I hope you can understand why I had to keep this from you," Ishan explained, his sincerity palpable as he laid bare the difficult truth.

My face froze in a mixture of disbelief and betrayal. Shock rendered me speechless, unable to form a coherent response. Seeing my stunned expression, Ishan continued with a somber tone.

"I had been considering various approaches to get close to you," he admitted, his voice steady yet filled with remorse. "Then Mitra disappeared, and I saw an opportunity to use your connection and get more information about your dad's involvement. That's why I got close to you."

He paused, the weight of his next words hanging heavily in the air.

"The day I visited your house, I installed hidden cameras and recorders in your father's office," Ishan confessed, his gaze unwavering. "I had no other choice. My own father was an investigating officer who was tracking your dad. He died in what was made to look like an accident, but it wasn't natural. Someone orchestrated it. I couldn't let history repeat itself. And now, knowing you're in danger, I had no option but to reveal everything and protect you."

His explanation was punctuated by a heavy silence, the gravity of his revelations sinking in as I struggled to comprehend the truth he had just unveiled.

I sat there, shattered, trying to absorb the torrent of information. "Aar... Aarav, are you alright?" Ishan asked, concern etched on his face.

Ishan moved closer, cupping my face with a gentle yet firm grip. "I know this is overwhelming, but I want you to know that I'm here for you. Trust me. We'll navigate this together. You're not alone." His voice was soothing, a reassuring presence in the midst of turmoil.

I looked into Ishan's eyes, searching for truth and finding it there. I took a deep breath, trying to steady myself. "Okay. What do we do now?" I asked, my voice resolute despite my inner turmoil.

Ishan squeezed my shoulder reassuringly. "First, we stay here for the night, away from any potential threats. Tomorrow, we'll figure out our next steps. We need to stay safe and gather more evidence to bring your father and his associates to justice."

I nodded, feeling a flicker of hope amid the chaos. With Ishan by my side, I felt a glimmer of strength returning. Together, we would face whatever came next, determined to uncover the truth and bring an end to the darkness that had overshadowed our lives.

CHAPTER VI

Guardian's Promise

As we lay in the dimly lit hotel room, my voice trembled with uncertainty as I turned to Ishan. "Why are you helping me?"

"I believe it's my duty to protect you," Ishan said softly, his gaze filled with empathy and sincerity. He paused, gathering his thoughts before continuing, "But more than that, I... I care deeply about you."

I looked at him, my heart fluttering with a mixture of emotions. "Why do you care about me?" I asked, my voice revealing both curiosity and vulnerability.

"Because," Ishan began gently yet firmly, "the day I brought you home, you spoke from your heart, even before you knew who I was."

"So, you care about me just because I opened up?" I pressed, needing to understand the depth of his feelings.

"I care about you because you showed me who you truly are, what you truly desire," Ishan replied with a tender smile. "You said you don't seek wealth, a grand house, or extravagant luxuries, but simply a heart to love and cherish. That kind of sincerity is rare and beautiful."

Ishan's eyes held mine, and I felt a connection that went beyond words. "Honestly, Aarav, I've been watching you for months. I needed an opening to interact with you and, in the meantime, I was trying to understand you more. I realized something was off about you. As far as the responses collected by my colleagues, it was too negative. You often seemed distant, avoiding meaningful conversations, and there were times when your temper

25

flared unexpectedly. You were sometimes overly critical of others, and it seemed like you were pushing people away. But I was more interested in finding out the reasons behind your negativity.

It was at that time I got a call from a colleague that you were at the bar. I saw a different Aarav that night, one who burst into tears in the washroom, thinking nobody was there. You acted cool with your friends, laughing and joking as if everything was fine, but in that brief moment of vulnerability, I realized something was burning inside you.

When you finally opened up to me, it gave me a new picture of who you are. I smiled to myself, thinking, 'Oh my God, how simple you are.' The things you said you didn't want that night were things I barely had, but the things you said you wanted, I had in abundance. That was my card to enter into your heart. But as I started knowing you more, my initial curiosity turned into affection, and at some point, it became love.

I realized that you have a beautiful heart when you put your whole trust in me to investigate your missing ex's case.

I am so sorry that I turned you down before. I genuinely had no choice. My intentions were never to hurt you, Aarav. I was trying to do my job while grappling with my feelings for you. I know it doesn't excuse my actions, but I hope you can understand the difficult position I was in."

His words washed over me, resonating deeply within my soul. Ishan's sincerity and understanding were like a balm to my wounded spirit, offering reassurance and a sense of belonging I had longed for. In that moment, amidst the uncertainties and challenges we faced, I found myself drawn closer to him, appreciating the depth of his care and the genuine connection we shared.

My expression softened, my thoughts drifting to a more somber realization. "No one has ever said anything like that to me, not even Mitra."

"That's because no one took the time to truly understand you," Ishan responded, his voice filled with empathy.

"You're right," I admitted quietly. "Do you know how lonely and troubled I've been?"

"I understand," Ishan said softly, reaching out to comfort me.

In a few moments of silence, Ishan continued, "Aarav, can I ask you something?" His tone turned serious, his eyes searching mine.

I nodded slowly, sensing the weight of the question to come.

"Will you be okay when the investigation team arrests your dad?" His concern was palpable. "You know the repercussions, the media attention it will bring."

I swallowed hard, my throat tightening with emotion. "As long as you're with me, I'll be okay. Please don't leave me. I need you."

"I won't leave you, I promise," Ishan reassured me, his voice steady and comforting.

"Ishan... Can I come closer, lie with you?" I hesitated, seeking reassurance once more.

"Of course," Ishan responded gently, opening his arms. "Let me hold you. Just relax and sleep peacefully. I'm right here with you."

With Ishan's comforting embrace, I slowly drifted into a peaceful sleep, my worries momentarily eased by the presence of someone who understood and cared deeply for me.

CHAPTER VII

Unraveling Shadows

As Varun awaited a lead on the involvement of Udham Sharma, his anticipation grew. He had strategically placed a GPS tracker under Udham Sharma's car to track his movements, hoping it would provide clues about Mitra's whereabouts and Udham's potential involvement in her disappearance. Varun knew the stakes were high, and every move needed to be executed with precision to keep me and himself safe while uncovering the truth.

Meanwhile, Udham Sharma, alerted to the surveillance on him, took immediate action. He instructed his assistant to wrap up matters swiftly and scolded them for mistakenly choosing Mitra. He also ordered them to keep a close watch on me and my newfound friend Varun. Udham Sharma never imagined his own son would turn against him by searching for his ex-girlfriend Mitra. Had it not been for my actions, Udham Sharma might never have been caught.

Udham Sharma's urgency suggested he was aware of potential threats to his secrecy and was taking preemptive measures to protect his interests.

The clock read 2:30 AM when Ishan's phone buzzed on the nightstand, its sharp ring breaking the silence of the night. He answered groggily, but the voice on the other end snapped him to attention.

"Ishan, we've got a lead on the warehouse. It's located in a remote area near the sea. We need to move now," his colleague's
urgent voice crackled through the line.

Ishan glanced at me. I was sleeping soundly beside him. Not wanting to disturb me, he scribbled a quick note and left it on the nightstand. "I got an emergency call. I'm on duty now. Please don't leave the room. Hope you will do that."

Slipping quietly out of the room, Ishan hurried to meet his team. The drive to the warehouse was tense, the night air thick with anticipation. They arrived at the remote location, only to find it heavily guarded. The warehouse loomed in the darkness, an impenetrable fortress.

"We can't just barge in," Ishan whispered to his team. "We need a plan."

Back at the hotel, my phone rang, waking

me from my sleep. The caller ID was unknown. I answered hesitantly, a chill running down my spine.

"Ishan is in danger," a distorted voice said. "You need to find him. Now."

Panic surged through me. Questions swirled in my mind: Who was calling? How did they know I was with Ishan? Where someone tailing us? And most importantly, was Ishan truly in danger? I glanced around the room and realized Ishan wasn't there. I called his phone, but there was no answer. In my haste, I missed the note on the nightstand and rushed out of the hotel, driven by fear for Ishan's safety.

The night air was cool and disorienting. My heart pounded as I hurried through the deserted streets, searching for any sign of

Ishan. Suddenly, a black car pulled up beside me, and two men grabbed me, forcing me inside. The door slammed shut, and they sped off into the night.

At my father's mansion, I was dragged inside and thrown into a dimly lit room. My dad stood there, a smug look on his face.

"I know where you were and with whom," Udham began, his voice cold and commanding. "That young police officer you care so much about? He's in my custody. If you want him to stay alive, you will do exactly as I say."

My heart sank. "Dad, how can you be this cruel? I never imagined you could be so heartless. Please, can you stop this madness?" I pleaded, my voice breaking.

Udham's expression hardened, but there was a flicker of something unreadable in his eyes. "You don't understand. Everything I do, I do for our family. That officer is meddling in affairs that don't concern him. If you want to keep him alive, you will withdraw from this case and come back home."

I shook my head, tears streaming down my face. "Dad, this isn't about family. This is about power and control. You're hurting innocent people, including the one I care. I can't stand by and let this happen."

Udham stepped closer, his eyes narrowing. "You will do as I say, or Ishan will pay the price. I have the power to end this. Choose wisely."

Meanwhile, at the warehouse, Ishan and his team formulated a plan to infiltrate the building. They needed to find a weak point in the security. As they scouted the perimeter, Ishan's phone buzzed with a message.

CHAPTER VIII

The Showdown

The investigation into Udham Sharma's trafficking ring had been long and arduous. Months of surveillance, wiretapping, and undercover operations had led the police to this critical moment. Every lead had been meticulously followed, every clue painstakingly pieced together to form a damning case against Sharma and his network. The officers had infiltrated the ring at various levels, posing as buyers, middlemen, and even potential recruits, gathering crucial intelligence that painted a horrifying picture of the trafficking operation.

It started with a tip from an informant, a former victim who had managed to escape the clutches of the traffickers. Her information had led the police to a web of deceit and cruelty that spanned multiple countries. The victims, often young girls from impoverished backgrounds, were lured with promises of jobs or education, only to be sold into a life of exploitation and misery. The traffickers were ruthless, using threats, violence, and drugs to control their victims.

As the investigation progressed, the team faced numerous challenges. There were moments of frustration when leads went cold, and times of danger when their undercover operatives were nearly discovered. The ring had high-level connections, making it difficult to trust even within the force. But the officers pressed on, driven by the resolve to dismantle this heinous operation and bring the perpetrators to justice.

The evidence they gathered was damning. Recorded conversations, intercepted shipments, and testimonies from rescued victims formed a solid case. The surveillance footage showed the faces of those involved, their callousness evident in every transaction. Financial records traced the flow of money, revealing the staggering profits made from the suffering of countless innocent lives.

Finally, after months of preparation, the police were ready to act. They had mapped out the entire operation, identifying key locations and individuals. The warehouse on the outskirts of the city was identified as a central hub where the trafficked girls were held before being shipped off to various destinations. The raid was planned with military precision, involving multiple teams and coordination with other law enforcement agencies.

The warehouse loomed ahead, a dark and foreboding structure shrouded in secrecy. Ishan and his team moved stealthily, their eyes scanning the perimeter for any sign of weakness in the security. They needed a plan, and they needed one fast.

As they scouted the area, Ishan's phone buzzed with a notification. He glanced at it and saw a missed call from me. His heart pounded, but he couldn't call back now; his phone was on silent mode to avoid detection.

The team continued their silent advance, but their progress was interrupted by the sound of a car approaching the warehouse. Ishan peered through the darkness and his breath caught in his throat. It was me, my face concealed but recognizable by my distinctive clothes.

"Aarav," Ishan whispered, his mind racing. He signaled to his team. "We have to move. Now."

Ishan's mind raced. My presence meant the stakes were higher than ever. Ishan and his team urgently requested their superior officers to deploy additional forces. They couldn't afford to fail. He signaled for reinforcements, calling for additional forces to back them up. The situation had escalated into a critical juncture.

My mind was a whirlwind of fear and determination. Why did I leave the hotel? What if Ishan was already hurt? The thought of losing him drove me forward, despite the danger. I had to find him.

Inside the warehouse, I was being held hostage by my father's men. Udham Sharma had set a trap, knowing Ishan would risk everything to save me. He ordered his men to maintain a tight watch on the premises, ready for any attempt at a rescue.

His breath quickened, muscles tensing with anticipation as he signaled to his team. With precise coordination, they moved swiftly into position, reinforced by the arrival of more police personnel. They braced themselves for a confrontation, fully aware of the need to act decisively and swiftly in the unfolding situation.

As the operation unfolded, a surge of adrenaline coursed through my veins. The orchestrated assault on the warehouse's main entrance marked the beginning of a dangerous dance with fate. The police, armed and determined, breached the doors, a flashbang grenade casting an eerie glow that pierced the darkness within. The sudden burst of light momentarily blinded our adversaries, providing a crucial advantage.

Gunfire erupted, the sharp reports echoing off the walls of the cavernous space. Ishan, leading the charge with unwavering focus, navigated through the chaos with calculated precision. His movements were swift, methodical, a testament to his training and resolve.

Amidst the turmoil, my eyes locked onto Ishan as he approached the center of the room where I was held captive, bound to a chair and surrounded by armed men. Relief flooded over me at the sight of him, a beacon of hope in the midst of uncertainty.

But the respite was short-lived. Udham Sharma's men, fiercely loyal and unwavering in their allegiance, retaliated with equal force. The air crackled with tension, each moment fraught with the uncertainty of survival.

As Ishan and his team engaged the enemy, I couldn't help but wonder about the outcome. Would we emerge victorious, or would this be the end of the road? My thoughts raced, my heart pounding in sync with the gunfire that reverberated around me. But one thought burned brighter than the rest – the resolve to save Mitra, no matter the cost.

Just as Ishan reached me, a shot rang out. I spun around, my heart dropping as I saw a gunman aiming at Ishan. Before I could think, I lunged forward, pushing Ishan out of the way. The bullet hit me below the left shoulder, the impact knocking me to the ground.

"Aarav!" Ishan shouted, his voice filled with anguish.

Another police officer immediately neutralized the gunman, who fell to the ground, lifeless. Ishan rushed to my side, his hands trembling as he checked the wound. Blood seeped through my shirt, but I was conscious.

Ishan cradled Aarav in his arms, his heart pounding with a mix of fear and relief. The chaos around them faded as his focus narrowed on the injured man before him. Aarav winced but managed a weak smile, his eyes locking onto Ishan's.

"You came," I whispered, my voice strained.

"Of course I did," Ishan replied, his voice choked with emotion. "I couldn't lose you."

The medics arrived swiftly, their efficiency a welcome sight. They moved with practiced precision, assessing my wound and preparing him for transport. Ishan stood back, his fists clenched, helpless to do more than watch as they stabilized me.

"We need to get him to a hospital," one of the medics said, glancing at Ishan. "He's lost a lot of blood."

Ishan nodded, his resolve firm. "I'll follow you."

As I was carried out on a stretcher, Ishan turned to his team. "Secure the warehouse. Make sure every corner is checked. We can't leave any stone unturned."

The team moved quickly, their professionalism undeterred by the emotional intensity of the situation. They swept through the warehouse, ensuring no one was left behind and collecting evidence to solidify the case against Udham Sharma and his network.

"You're going to be okay," Ishan said, his voice steady despite the turmoil inside him.

The warehouse was secured as the remaining guards were subdued. Udham Sharma was apprehended, his plans thwarted. The police moved quickly to search the premises, uncovering a network of hidden rooms and locked doors.

Among the rescued were Mitra and ten other girls, all victims of the trafficking ring. They were terrified but safe, their ordeal finally over. The dimly lit room they had been confined to was now filled with the bright lights of freedom, but their eyes remained haunted, shadows of their harrowing experience.

Outside, the police discovered a ship harbored nearby, intricately linked to the trafficking operation. The vessel loomed ominously, a floating prison that had carried countless girls into darkness. As officers boarded the ship, a sense of dread hung in the air, thick and suffocating.

In the belly of the ship, they found a container. Its metallic surface was cold to the touch, a stark contrast to the life it concealed.

As the doors creaked open, the officers were met with a scene that could only be described as a nightmare. The interior of the container was dimly lit by the harsh overhead lights of the ship, casting eerie shadows on the walls. The air inside was thick with a pungent mix of sweat, urine, and fear, a suffocating atmosphere that clung to the senses.

The girls inside the container were sprawled in various states of disarray, their bodies limp and unresponsive. Many were huddled together, seeking comfort in the closeness of another human being. Their clothes were tattered and soiled, barely clinging to their frail frames. The sharp outlines of their ribs and collarbones were painfully visible, a stark indication of prolonged starvation and neglect.

Eyes, glazed and vacant, stared out from gaunt faces. Some girls were semi-conscious, their heads lolling weakly as they fought to stay awake against the heavy sedation. Others lay completely still, their bodies unnaturally contorted in the cramped space. The floor of the container was a grim tableau of human suffering, littered with the detritus of their captivity—empty water bottles, scraps of food, and makeshift bedding.

Whimpers and soft cries filled the air, a chorus of despair that tugged at the hearts of the rescuers. The officers moved quickly yet gently, their expressions a mix of horror and determination. They called for medics, their voices urgent, as they began to lift the girls out of the container one by one.

As each girl was brought into the light, the extent of their ordeal became heartbreakingly clear. Many had bruises and cuts, some fresh and others in various stages of healing, testament to the abuse they had endured. Needle marks dotted their arms, evidence of the sedatives used to keep them compliant. The skin of some girls was pallid and clammy, a sign of dehydration and malnutrition.

The officers' hands were gentle as they wrapped the girls in blankets, offering them the first semblance of warmth and comfort they had felt in a long time. Tears glistened in the eyes of the rescuers, their hearts breaking at the sight of such profound suffering.

Outside the container, a triage area had been set up. Medical teams worked frantically to assess and treat the girls, their professional detachment strained by the overwhelming emotions of the moment. IV drips were set up, oxygen masks placed, and soft reassurances whispered in a multitude of languages.

The girls' reactions varied. Some clung desperately to their rescuers, seeking the comfort of human contact after so long in the dark. Others were unresponsive, their eyes staring blankly as they were carried to safety. A few sobbed uncontrollably, the release of pent-up fear and trauma flooding out in an uncontrollable torrent.

As the operation continued, the true scale of the trafficking ring's cruelty became painfully evident. The container, once a vessel of hope and dreams for these girls, had become a prison of unimaginable horrors. The officers, though seasoned and hardened by years of service, found themselves deeply affected by the sight before them.

In the aftermath, the girls would require extensive medical and psychological care to begin the long process of healing. But for now, they were safe. The darkness of their captivity had been pierced by the light of rescue, and as they were carried out of the container, a new chapter in their lives began—a chapter of hope, recovery, and, eventually, justice.

Udham Sharma and his men were arrested, their criminal empire dismantled.

The warehouse was thoroughly investigated, revealing the full extent of their heinous activities. The international trafficking ring was exposed, leading to a broader investigation by Interpol.

The main villain, Denzil D'zusa, became the subject of an intense manhunt, his name now synonymous with immorality and human suffering. The coordinated efforts of law enforcement agencies worldwide intensified, determined to bring him to justice.

This was it – the culmination of all their efforts. The moment they had worked tirelessly for. The chance to strike a blow against one of the most insidious criminal enterprises they had ever encountered. As they geared up for the raid, the gravity of the situation weighed heavily on their minds. They knew the risks but also the potential for saving lives and bringing justice to those who had suffered.

As the dawn broke, casting a soft light over the city, there was a renewed sense of hope. The darkness had been confronted, and though the battle was far from over, the light of justice had pierced through, bringing with it the promise of a brighter future.

CHAPTER IX

A Bond Forged in Adversity

As I was rushed to the hospital, Ishan stayed by my side, his heart heavy with worry. The ambulance sped through the city streets, sirens blaring. Ishan held my hand tightly, whispering words of comfort and encouragement, though his mind was racing with fear.

Upon arrival at the hospital, the medical team sprang into action. I was immediately taken into the operating room, leaving Ishan standing anxiously in the corridor. Time seemed to stretch endlessly as he paced back and forth, his thoughts consumed by the image of my pale face and the blood staining my clothes.

Finally, a doctor emerged from the operating room, pulling off his surgical mask. He approached Ishan, his expression serious but reassuring.

"We've managed to stabilize him," the doctor said. "The bullet missed any major organs, but it caused significant damage. He's going to need time to recover, but he's out of immediate danger."

Ishan let out a breath he hadn't realized he was holding. "Thank you, doctor. Can I see him?"

The doctor nodded. "He'll be moved to the intensive care unit shortly. You can see him once he's settled."

Minutes felt like hours as Ishan waited. Eventually, a nurse guided him to my room. Ishan entered quietly, his eyes immediately drawn to me lying on the hospital bed, surrounded by monitors and IV lines. His heart ached at the sight, but relief washed over him knowing that I was alive. The stringent ICU rules allowed Ishan only a brief five minutes with me, during which he held my hand tightly, whispering words of encouragement and love.

After what seemed like an eternity, Ishan reluctantly left the ICU, his mind filled with worry and hope. He paced the hospital corridor, waiting for any news of my condition. The next twenty-four hours dragged on, each moment weighed down by the uncertainty of my recovery. Finally, Ishan received the news that I had stabilized and was being transferred to a recovery room. It was a small but hopeful step forward in our journey to healing.

Ishan pulled a chair close to the bed and sat down, taking my hand in his. "You're going to be okay," he whispered, his voice trembling. "I'm here, and I'm not going anywhere."

My eyes fluttered open, my gaze meeting Ishan's. I tried to speak, but my voice was weak. Ishan gently shushed me.

"Don't try to talk," Ishan said softly. "Just rest. The doctors said you're going to be fine."

Tears welled up in my eyes, and I gave Ishan's hand a weak squeeze. "I was so scared," I whispered.

"I know," Ishan replied, his own eyes moist with unshed tears. "But you're safe now. We got through it together."

As the days passed, my condition steadily improved. Ishan rarely left my side, keeping vigil by my bed and offering constant support. The hospital staff began to know him by name, touched by his unwavering dedication.

One evening, as the sun set outside the hospital window, casting a warm glow over the room, I looked at Ishan with a mixture of gratitude and love. "Thank you for everything, Ishan. You saved my life."

Ishan smiled, brushing a stray lock of hair from my forehead. "We saved each other, remember? That's what we do."

I nodded, my eyes shining with emotion. "I love you, Ishan."

"I love you too," Ishan replied, leaning down to kiss my forehead gently. "And I'll always be here for you, no matter what."

As I continued to heal, our bond grew even stronger, forged in the fire of our shared ordeal. We knew that challenges still lay ahead, but we also knew we could face anything together. With that knowledge, we found a renewed sense of hope and determination, ready to embrace whatever the future held.

CHAPTER X

Dawn of a New Era

The capture of Udham Sharma indeed dominated the headlines, but it was the revelation of international involvement in human trafficking by Denzil D'zusa that truly captivated global attention. Media outlets worldwide lauded the Indian investigation team for their unwavering determination and swift action in dismantling such a far-reaching criminal network.

Furthermore, the investigation uncovered startling evidence implicating Udham Sharma in the intentional murder disguised as an accident of Ishan's father. This revelation added a new layer of darkness to Udham Sharma's already notorious legacy, further solidifying the gravity of his crimes and the impact of justice finally catching up with him.

Amidst the media frenzy, I became a focal point due to my father's notoriety. Despite being injured and hospitalized, the relentless scrutiny from the press was unyielding, exposing the darker side of media sensationalism. Cameras and journalists hounded me, eager for a glimpse of the son of the infamous Udham Sharma. However, I found solace in Ishan's unwavering support, which shielded me from the external chaos and provided a sanctuary of calm and love.

Meanwhile, Mitra, recovering from her own ordeal, realized the complexity of her involvement in the events that transpired, whether knowingly or unknowingly. Determined to make amends, she visited me in the hospital as soon as she was well enough. Her gratitude was heartfelt as she thanked both Ishan and me for our bravery and dedication.

"I owe my life to you both," Mitra said, her eyes filled with tears. "I can't begin to express how grateful I am."

I squeezed her hand. "We're just glad you're safe, Mitra. We couldn't have done it without each other."

I needed time to heal, both physically and emotionally. Once discharged from the hospital, Ishan brought me to his home and took on the role of my caretaker. The weeks passed, and under Ishan's attentive care, I slowly regained my strength. Our bond grew even deeper during this time, the shared experience further cementing our connection.

Two months had passed, and I, having made significant strides in my recovery, felt compelled to confront my tumultuous past. With Ishan steadfastly by my side, we made our way to the prison where my father, Udham Sharma, was confined. The atmosphere was thick with unspoken tension and unresolved emotions as we faced each other for the first time in years.

"I," Udham greeted quietly, his voice tinged with a mix of remorse and resignation. "I never wanted things to end this way. I'm sorry ."

As I looked at my father, conflicting emotions surged within me. Memories of my childhood, tainted now by the revelation of his crimes, collided with the need to understand his motivations.

"Dad," I started, my voice trembling with a mix of anger and sorrow. "Your choices have caused irreparable pain to countless people, including me. But I need to understand why you would do such a thing."

Udham's shoulders slumped further as he let out a deep sigh. His eyes, once filled with arrogance, now showed remorse and regret. "Power corrupts, my child," he muttered hoarsely. "I thought I was securing our future, protecting our legacy. But I lost sight of what truly matters."

My gaze hardened, betraying the turmoil within me. "When I needed my dad the most, I didn't realize you had taken away Ishan's dad—the man who means everything to me now."

Tears welled up in my eyes, anger bubbling beneath the surface. "Did you gain anything from destroying lives, Dad?" I demanded, my voice cracking with emotion. "You should pay for your crimes."

Udham Sharma, once a figure of authority and power, now sat before me broken and remorseful.

The weight of my words hung heavy in the air, and Udham's expression softened, guilt etched deeply into his features. "I'm sorry, Ishan," he muttered, his voice barely above a whisper. "For everything."

Ishan's presence beside me was a reminder of the profound impact Udham's actions had on his life. The pain he had inflicted upon Ishan, a dedicated police officer and a loving father, now mirrored the anguish I felt knowing the truth about my own father. Ishan's eyes bore into Udham with a mixture of sorrow and anger, his words cutting through the silence like a sharp blade.

"You took away my father when I needed him most," Ishan's voice cut through the stale air, his tone low but brimming with an unyielding resolve that echoed off the prison walls. "Your choices didn't just break families, Udham. They shattered lives—mine, Aarav's. Lives that will never be the same because of you. You will carry that weight for the rest of your days."

Udham Sharma met Ishan's unwavering gaze, his own eyes clouded with regret and guilt as the full impact of his actions weighed heavily upon him. The silence that followed was thick with the weight of unspoken truths and the harsh reality of irreversible consequences.

The visit ended with a palpable sense of closure, but the weight of our shared history lingered. As I turned away from Udham Sharma, I knew that forgiving him wouldn't erase the scars he had left on our lives. Yet, in confronting him, I had taken a crucial step toward reclaiming my own sense of peace and forging a path forward, guided by the lessons learned from both love and betrayal.

Returning to college marked a new beginning for me. The campus buzzed with curiosity about my recent experiences, but I faced it all with quiet resilience. Ishan's presence was a constant source of strength, and together we navigated this new chapter in my life.

As the days turned into weeks, I found a renewed sense of purpose. I embraced my studies with a vigor I hadn't felt in years, and my relationship with Ishan blossomed, providing me with the love and support I had always yearned for. The shadows of the past gradually receded, replaced by a future filled with hope and possibility.

Mitra, too, found her own path to healing. She remained close to me and Ishan, our shared history binding us in a unique and enduring friendship. The experiences we had faced together forged an unbreakable bond, a testament to our resilience and the power of love and forgiveness.

One sunny afternoon, Ishan and I took a stroll through a park near our home. The vibrant flowers and chirping birds seemed to mirror our renewed spirits. We sat on a bench, watching the world go by, content in each other's presence.

"Aarav," Ishan began, turning to face me, "I know the past few months have been incredibly tough, but seeing you recover and thrive means everything to me."

I smiled, my eyes reflecting the warmth of my feelings. "I couldn't have done it without you, Ishan. You've been my rock through all of this."

Ishan took my hand, squeezing it gently. "We're a team, Aarav. We'll face everything together, no matter what."

I turned to Ishan, my eyes shining with deep emotion. "Ishan, you've brought so much light into my life. Before I knew it, you became my everything. I see the God in you, in your kindness and strength. Thank you for coming into my life."

Ishan's heart swelled with love as he gazed at me. He gently pulled me into a tender embrace, our foreheads touching. "Aarav, you've transformed my world too. Every day, I'm grateful for the moment our paths crossed."

As we sat there, surrounded by the beauty of nature and the promise of a new beginning, we felt an overwhelming sense of gratitude for each other and for the life we were building together. Challenges would undoubtedly come, but we were ready to face them, armed with our love and the unshakeable strength of our partnership.

In the end, my life was transformed. I had faced unimaginable challenges and emerged stronger, surrounded by those who cared for me deeply. With Ishan by my side, I felt a sense of completeness and joy I had never known before. Together, we were ready to embrace whatever the future held, confident in our love and the enduring bond that had been forged through our shared journey.

CHAPTER XI

I see God in him

Ishan came into my life like an unexpected miracle. A total stranger, he arrived uninvited but became my steadfast anchor in a storm of uncertainty. His presence has transformed my existence in ways I never imagined possible. Step by step, he conquered my heart and soul, becoming the very essence of my strength and hope.

When I was lost and desperate for help, he appeared seemingly out of nowhere, a beacon of light in my darkest hour. The weight of my father's menacing influence threatened to crush me, but Ishan stood by my side, a shield against the shadows. His courage and determination protected me when I couldn't protect myself.

When I was hospitalized, Ishan worried about me with an intensity that brought him to tears. His care and dedication were unwavering. He stayed by my bedside, offering comfort and reassurance with every gentle touch. When I needed a place to call home, he opened his doors without hesitation, welcoming me into his life with open arms. In moments of sorrow, when tears fell like rain, he became my pillow, absorbing my pain and giving me the solace I so desperately needed.

His heart, pure and unyielding, became my sanctuary. He offered his love freely, understanding me in ways I never thought possible. With Ishan, I found a connection deeper than words, a bond forged in the fires of adversity and compassion. He gave me his heart, and in doing so, he became my everything.

I never imagined that I would have someone who loves me so profoundly. I find myself questioning whether I deserve this boundless love and compassion. When I think about the cruelty my dad inflicted on his life, my heart sinks with pain. The contrast between the darkness of my father's actions and the light of Ishan's love is almost unbearable. And yet, here he is, steadfast and true, a living testament to the power of love and forgiveness.

In my life, Ishan is more than a man; he is an embodiment of divinity, a living, breathing miracle. His presence is a testament to the power of love and faith, a reminder that even in the bleakest times, hope can be found. I adore him, admire him, and treasure him with every fiber of my being.

Perhaps he came into my life for a reason, a divine purpose beyond my understanding. But now, I cannot fathom a life without him. The warmth of his embrace, the depth of his love, and the care he showers upon me are more than I could ever ask for. He is my sanctuary, my protector, my heart.

In Ishan, I see the very essence of God, an incarnation of grace and love sent to guide and cherish me. For me, there is no need to thank the heavens, for in Ishan, God himself walks by my side. In other words, I see God in him.

Have you ever imagined having a person like that in your life? Or perhaps, if you are truly fortunate, do you already have someone who embodies such profound love and devotion? I feel incredibly fortunate to have him by my side.

The Final Judgment

In the quiet solitude of his prison cell, Udham Sharma found himself confined not only by the physical bars but also by the weight of remorse and regret that hung heavy upon his soul. Once a feared figure of power and influence, he now grappled with the stark reality of his choices, each decision etched into the fabric of his existence. The journey from orchestrating a vast criminal empire to facing the consequences of his actions had stripped away the veneer of invincibility he had meticulously crafted over the years. "In the silence of confinement, I confront the echoes of my choices," he reflected, his voice a whisper against the stark walls.

Meanwhile, amidst the acclaim and accolades for dismantling Udham Sharma's criminal network, Ishan stood tall, his gaze always drawn to the one who had redefined his purpose: Aarav. Beyond the headlines and the public praise, Ishan found true fulfillment in the quiet moments shared with Aarav. From the relentless pursuit of justice to becoming Aarav's steadfast protector and lover, Ishan's journey had been marked by unwavering courage and unyielding compassion. "Love, protect, heal—beyond duty, lies the heart's true calling," he mused, his thoughts drifting to the profound bond they shared.

And in the heart of Aarav's odyssey through darkness and light, resilience and redemption intertwined in a testament to the human spirit's enduring strength. Emerging from the shadows of his father's legacy, Aarav bore the scars of his past as badges of honor, each marking a milestone on his journey of self-discovery and healing.

"Scars tell stories of battles won, hearts healed, and futures reclaimed," he often reflected, his eyes filled with a quiet determination and a profound sense of gratitude for the love and support that had guided him through the darkest of times.

Their paths, though divergent, carried lessons from their shared journey. Udham Sharma, once consumed by the allure of power, now faced the stark reality of his choices. Ishan, steadfast in his compassion, embraced his role not only as a dedicated police officer but as a pillar of strength and unwavering support for Aarav. And Aarav, embodying resilience and forgiveness, looked toward the horizon with unwavering hope, his spirit forged anew through the transformative power of love and redemption.

"In the crucible of darkness, hearts found light. In forgiveness, souls discovered freedom. And in the embrace of love, they found the strength to rise," their intertwined stories echoed through the corridors of time—a testament to the enduring capacity of the human spirit to heal, grow, and find light even in the darkest of times.

Thus, amidst the echoes of their trials and triumphs, their lives intertwined—a profound narrative of resilience, redemption, and the transformative power of love.